AN APPROACH TO BLACK

Emily Jeremiah holds an MA in Creative Writing from Goldsmiths, University of London, and was awarded Arts Council funding to work on her debut novella, *Blue Moments* (Valley Press, 2020). A professor at Royal Holloway, University of London, she is the author of three academic books. With her Finnish mother, Fleur Jeremiah, she has co-translated five novels, one of which, *White Hunger* by Aki Ollikainen (Peirene Press), was longlisted for the Man Booker International Prize 2016. She has translated two selections of poetry for Waterloo Press. A volume of poems by Pentti Saarikoski, co-translated with Fleur Jeremiah, appeared in 2020 (Norvik Press).

ALSO BY EMILY JEREMIAH

Blue Moments

An Approach to Black

Emily Jeremiah

REFLEX PRESS

First published in 2021 by Reflex Press
Abingdon, Oxfordshire, OX14 3SY
www.reflex.press

A CIP catalogue record of this book is available from the British Library.

ISBN: 978-1-9161115-8-5

1 3 5 7 9 10 8 6 4 2

Printed and bound in Great Britain by
Imprint Digital, Upton Pyne, Exeter

Front cover image *The Door* by Helene Schjerfbeck, 1884.
Courtesy of The Finnish National Gallery.

Back cover image by Sweet Art/Shutterstock.com.

www.reflex.press/an-approach-to-black/

There is her self, in her own words.

His books do well. The picture-book idyll of our house, a wooden ship in its meadow sea, sprawling ever more as new rooms are tacked on, year after year. How pretty it is, with striped rugs and cheerful hangings, begonias flowering on sills and shelves, rosy children, pegged-up laundry. The narrator of my artist-husband's illustrated tales is our daughter. A sweet conceit. And I? A bonnet, a pale cheek, a few stray tendrils of hair. 'My mother used to paint, too, but now she looks after us and the house.'

He came from Paris today. The children clustered round him. We ate cinnamon buns under the whispering leaves of the birch, in view of the lake.

I asked him whom had he seen, and I could picture them, crowded into rooms, huddled over stoves, a brazen nude shivering on the table. Albert, of course. Kalle. Boulevards, and parks, and cafés, and attics, and coarse red wine.

'And Helena?' I asked.

The light of the oil-lamp flickered as I sat darning, the children in bed. There is colour all around, for he loves it. Red, especially. That combats the dark of the evenings, a little. In the day, it screams at me. Green, I love; the colour of hope.

The green pear in Helena's painting is recumbent, nonchalant, its stalk woody and rough. The green is speckled, stippled, lined with swerving brown arcs. At the base of the pear sits a dark rosette.

As well as red, Eino loves fine shirts and waistcoats, and tobacco, and cognac, and evenings in restaurants and theatres. And travel, movement.

A bright blue sky, and the children went to the lake. And a letter from Helena. She tells of a prize she won – her painting was praised as daring and masculine.

I remember us as young students. It wasn't so long ago. There was that evening gathering in a crowded room. Helena was talking to another student, gesticulating fiercely. The man I was sitting with tickled my cheek with a feather. He had been to Italy. I was envious. That was Eino: mop of brown curls and laughing eyes. Like a kitten, or a squirrel – that quickness, that zest.

Music, dancing. Crunchy snow afterwards and I remember imagining myself in Italy, in a white dress, and the zestful eyes looking at me.

Secret notes from Eino after that and a secret radiance about me through the winter. And then marriage and a frothy white dress, and the church garlanded with flowers, and a long table under birch trees. I was hot and dazed in the sun, bitten by mosquitoes. Helena had gone to Italy.

She is here. I watched and waited, saw them from afar coming from the station in the trap. Her eyes pierced me, as from a stern portrait, when she came in. 'Anna,' she said simply. She is a picture of herself. What do I mean? She is herself. I am myself, too, of course. The children were shy. 'Come in,' I said. But she already was in. I felt like a child.

I ushered her to the table: flowers in a vase, two kinds of cake, pretty cups. 'Sit,' I said. 'Tell me about Paris!'

'Oh, Paris...' she answered, almost mockingly.

I lifted my cup, felt myself frown. Was she mocking me, or herself?

She seemed to relent. 'Good,' she stated. 'My painting was well received, as I wrote...' She bit her lip, as if ashamed. Her long fingers played with the handle of her pretty, porcelain cup, which didn't match her severity. I wondered if the same went for the whole house – was she out of place here?

I nodded permission at Olavi to leave the table; he wiped his jammy mouth with his sleeve. Eino began to talk of his plans for the following day, about a dealer he was to meet.

By the lake, I asked her if it was good to be home, and she said, 'Home?' Always this pushing away. The sky was a brooding grey. The children were throwing pebbles into the water, running around the shore – too cold to swim. The fullness of them.

'Finland,' I said with a harsh tone, and she looked right at me. A crow cawed, and we both looked at it, then at each other again. The sight of the black bird in the birch tree, the jet feathers, the green fall of foliage, took us both briefly away from the push-pull between us.

Wisps of brown hair, escaped from their bun, played around her face, in stern three-quarters profile. I would like to paint her, I thought then, with her face angled just that way, against a silver-grey background.

'I'm not sure that home is a place for me,' she said, frowning. She still walks in that odd, slightly jerky way; an ungainly, endearing puppet. She was wearing a dark, plain dress. She does not like people to look at her.

‘What is it then?’ I asked. I looked straight ahead, at the house. Red-painted, with white-bordered windows, surrounded by trees. My home. The children ran on ahead, whooping and crowing. They sent birds shooting up out of the trees.

Helena finally responded: ‘I don’t know. A feeling, perhaps...’

‘And where are you living now?’ I asked.

‘I will stay with Liisa, at least for six months or so. And then I hope to go to Provence for a time. The Englishwoman I lodged with in Paris has friends there.’

I learnt that this Englishwoman was called Margaret. She was from a well-to-do family that despaired of her passion for art and her failure to marry.

Helena suddenly sat down on a mossy rock and looked up.

‘You don’t paint now?’ she pushed.

I stared down at her.

*

Black beetles crawling. Lampblack. Visions, are they? They are Life, but what aspect? The teeming, the abject, the uncontrollable. Creepy-crawlying up the bed frame. Nurses rustle about. I am sack-like, sagging, before the upright doctor. Yes, sir. I stare, and I speak.

Lampblack. Ochre, sinopia, malachite. Beetles beetling. Colours.

I have to get out of here. My children. I should be under the birch tree. Not here. But when I make to leave, I can’t. And I know I have to be well-behaved so they will let me go out, to the garden at least, so I mustn’t pummel the door as I have been doing. It will do no good; they will restrain me in that jacket again.

But I have to try. I can't let them keep me here. 'Please may I go out?' I try calling. Please, please, please. There is no reply.

How is this to help, this confinement? When will this cease? Will time cease? Will I be back where I started, when this is over – if it is ever over – or will I be in some other time?

They make me vomit. I am to cough out all the nastiness. Bile comes up; does the badness? I want the badness to go, too.

I try to leave, again and again. I don't know how many times. I can see marks on my hands and wrist. I must have tried many times.

I know not to do so now, but I still sometimes ask. I can't help it, still hoping I might have an effect on one of my gaolers, that my husband might yet retrieve me and release me.

They put me in that jacket in which I cannot move. I am barely a person. I am barely myself. I am to behave well. If I behave well, I might be allowed to be myself.

We are soaked in large vats as if to dissolve us.

Breathe, breathe, breathe.

Heart goes boom, boom, boom.

The nurses are imperturbable, even thriving on my pleading glances, so I become stony, or try to. Succeed as well, or think I do, sometimes. Who knows? The self, crumbling, toppling in on itself.

Time has stopped. Or has it? It just passes, marked only by the routine of this place, the institution to which I have been carted, a recalcitrant beast. Bright and white here. Shadows stark, on sunny days. They watch me all the time. I behave well. I can even go out into the garden now.

The garden is beautiful, and the bay. I have to watch out for the birds. Crows are sometimes menacing, then the menace passes and they are fine, even good. Magpies are bold, cheeky birds. But they let me be. They represent what they represent. All birds are good – signs that my attention is being rewarded, indications of beauty and life in this world.

Sunshine is good, a blessing after the winter. I felt it on my face today, or the other day. I was amazed by the air, the sea, the trees, the birds. 'Oh, it's beautiful,' I even said to someone.

Dare I hope that I shall go outside again? Dare I hope that I shall live again, beyond this existence in this cell? Nighttimes I am pursued by visions and wake up clammy. These are visions; by day, I know it. By night I am the subject of an exhibition, open to the world, and everyone is laughing, or grimacing with disgust – such a pitiful exhibit, laid out flat like a fish there. Such a – nothing, somebody says, a man's voice.

What does this do for the nation? Someone else asks. For the people?

I lie squirming beneath their gaze. I wish not to exist or to be transformed into another substance – water, air – so as to slip or waft away, to be unseen. I am nothing in any case.

I am nothing. Is that not what I was saying, back home, before I was brought here, in accordance with the law and all that is decent? I cannot remember. Where are the children? I am not nothing to them. I am something, but of what substance am I?

I look at my arms in the moonlight. They are pale, like marble. I put them round me. I am still warm, alive, not a sculpture, not inanimate. I live and breathe, and perhaps I'll get out of here, perhaps I'll resume my life, a life, at some point in time.

But what is life? Crawling life, matter. Whose is it? Who has control over it? I remember painting, that sense of my will, of creation, that drive towards permanence.

And colour: I remember colour, here in this bleached-out place, in the light of the moon. Colour, an approach to black. I get up and wander round. I have this little bit of space, at least; they allow me this, now that I'm good. I wonder what will happen to me. Is there a record of this? The doctor makes notes. Will there be a record of me, of my existence?

The bark of the birch tree is black and white. Bird. What kind? Magpie. Thief! But leaves swishing. Green shifting in the sun. Interleaving leaves, and she rocks herself, clasping herself, lulled, lulled, somehow hopeful, pitifully small before Nature, the World, but still daring to cling to Life, and rocking, remembering being mothered – daring to do that too – and remembering too mothering, her sweet and beautiful children.

Go back inside. I, not she. I go back inside.

Now I paint most days. I feel clearer. The doctor says it makes me calmer. I was already so calm!

When it's fine, I go outside, for I am permitted to paint outside, finally, and alone, watched from a distance, like the Impressionists, like my friend Elin does in Brittany. I am allowed to work outside without fear that I will tear off and plunge myself into the water.

En plein air. Full air. Air full of expectation, for me, and leaves rustling, swishing in the breeze. I will paint this water, the ripples, the glints, the green of it; and the trees that border it; and the rowing boat just so, seeming to point into water, hopefully, from its station by the jetty.

Permanence, of course, is an illusion, but one we pursue, rather tenaciously, through framing and through institutionalisation of other kinds. Glass cases, mounts, bindings, boxes, containers.

Here – strapped gowns, and vats; uniforms, starched. The dark men, the light women. Containment and contrast. This is how it is. But one shouldn't see it, no.

But I do. And I can still paint! They allow me that, and my hand does still lift the brush, and I still do smell the paint, and the turps, and I still mix the colours, and...

At night, the moon beams down. Lunatic, lunar tick. Howling at the moon. One man here does that. They say he is a writer, that he showed great promise. Who said that? Eino? He came. I hope the children were not with him – not here. I hope they are safe and happy with their... I? With me? But I am... I? Here.

The doctor makes notes in his black notebook. He takes the time to chat to me today. Now I'm different, not exposing myself or wailing. Oh no, I'm an artist. I think the doctor finds this amusing.

I don't think my husband finds it amusing. He doesn't like to talk about it, when he comes on his visits. Today he is wearing the thick fur coat he bought in Russia. It is cold outside now. He gets up and walks over to the window when I ask him what is showing in Paris.

'I don't know, dear,' he says, turning round.

'There was that painting, of a wounded soldier.' I struggle to see it, but all I come up with is a sketch. Somebody drew me a sketch.

'Don't worry, my dear,' he says. He says that all the time now. 'My dear.' Not my name. It seems to be easier for him.

Then he says: 'The doctor says you are really much better these days. You make conversation. You are calm, and you seem content.'

I nod.

On the ward is a woman who sits statue-like and calls out, in a warbling yet penetrating voice, 'Come, come, there, there, you took my soul away, you took my sight away.' Her eyes are milky, and her hair, whitened before its time, forms a plaited crown about her head. In her white gown, she is both waif-like and holy-seeming. She sometimes flops in the chair, arms flapping to the side, exhaling loudly; at other times, calling out, she flails her arms. But always there is something mesmerising about her. I don't want to know her story, all the stories.

They don't talk, the patients, among themselves, beyond fragments, in the shuffling queue for 'baths'.

But they do speak, don't they? I should listen. Another patient attaches great significance to numbers, and hearing one mentioned will linger over it: three score years and ten, or statistics she had heard tell of via the newspaper. Numbers of ships; amount of rainfall. It is deadly dull. Another sings: uncanny airs. It makes you mad, being here. But she was mad, anyway. But was she? But what is madness?

And so on, the exhausting loop. No outwards, no elsewhere, no onwards.

But now I have painting. Where is Helena? She has gone, hasn't she? Is she...? Oh, they would have told me, wouldn't they?

Who took my sight away? Who took my soul away? No one!

There is a doctor who makes notes.

The doctor was tall, upright, dressed in black.

Anna S. was a little restless today. She had green-grey eyes, which arrested him, as he asked his usual questions, made his usual notes.

He got up, towered darkly over her as she sagged palely in her strappy gown. Hair escaped from her bun.

He prescribed immersion in water. The baths were large vats, and into them were placed patients' recalcitrant bodies. Oh, the body, with its openings and effluents and embarrassments, its ongoing revelations, its decrepitude and decay.

But Dr Salomsson strolled along the shore, between water and yellow building, fine figure of a man, he, and he believed in this dunking of the unruly bodies, especially the female ones. He stooped to pick up a feather.

He was an analyst, though; he knew enough to ask questions and wonder at his satisfaction in this procedure. And keep on strolling along the lakeside, puffing out clouds of violet smoke from his thick, black, stiff pipe.

Later he put sugar in his tea using silver tongs, steam swirling and rising from the cup. Luxury. His wife sat opposite him, neat skull encasing her brain, hair smooth and ordered.

A ship sounded its horn from the nearby harbour, and his thoughts turned to Anna S., again.

There are others in the future who will try to make sense of things, and of themselves.

From: Anja Honkasalo, *From the Doll's House to the Mad House: Middle-Class Women as Mental Health Patients in L., 1841–1918*

Anna S. was admitted to L. in 1890 and was confined there for five months. According to her husband, the well-known artist Eino S., his wife was 'refusing to engage in normal marital activities'. She also expressed 'an unnatural desire for independence'. According to her husband, she had repeatedly expressed the desire to travel, 'to London or Paris'. She had been neglecting her duties as a mother and sitting listlessly in one room. On other occasions, she was 'unnaturally' high-spirited and went about singing and dancing.

The trigger for this latest outburst appears to have been a visit made by a friend of the patient, Helena W. According to a letter sent by her husband to his friend, fellow artist Pietari Johanssen, this visit had left her unusually on edge. She had neglected her duties as a wife and mother even more than before and continued to express wild and unrealistic desires to travel.

We know little of Anna S.'s life before her marriage to Eino, whom she met in Helsinki in 1887.

The treatment prescribed to Anna S. consisted initially of absolute rest. It is likely that common treatments such as baths and emetics were used. Only mild exercise was permitted and was to be supervised by a nurse. Visits were strongly discouraged; only Eino was permitted to come, once a month. When the patient grew restless or aggressive, she was restrained: strapped to her bed, as records show us.

According to these records, Anna did not initially respond well to treatment. She was often 'restless and aggressive'. On more than one occasion, she attempted to run away, in common with Anna P., whose case was described in Chapter 1.

Anna was eventually permitted to paint, and according to her records, this activity soothed her. By this time, Dr Salomsson had come to the institution, and it appears that it is largely thanks to his influence that 'artistic' patients like Anna S. were allowed to practise such activities.

Following her release from L., it is believed Anna S. was first housed in a property belonging to her family, in the care of a local woman, then moved to the hospital at P., where she lived until her death of pneumonia at the age of forty.

Notes towards *Painting Silence: The Life and Work of Anna S.*

The life and work of Anna S. has been largely overlooked [footnote here – bare biog. facts]. This overlooking [rephrase] stems from three main reasons: firstly, her marriage to Eino S., the well-known painter and illustrator, popularly known as 'the Carl Larsson of Finland' [footnote – find references, give details of his main works]. Secondly, her small output, much of which was produced when she was in her early twenties [details]. Thirdly, and related to these points: her gender. Anna S. has tended to be lumped together with other female artists of the same period, dubbed the Golden Age of Finnish art, and considered 'minor' [put below?]. Here, through analysis of its technique and themes, I will demonstrate the overlooked significance of her work, arguing that it forms a distinct and noteworthy contribution to golden-age Finnish art.

Anna's union with S. meant that Anna has largely been referred to in the infrequent accounts of her life that do exist [rephrase] as 'the wife of Eino S.' [give refs]. Occasionally there have been references to her own training and status as a painter (Bergman; Järvinen – check and find page references), but even here, there is no attempt to characterise her work, or give an account of it...

The woman opened the door. Emma, he forced himself to remember. Bad with names – because of his narcissism? That's what *he* would have said, Billy, his ex. Billy, whose voice he kept hearing, belittling him, questioning him.

'Hei!' she said. Jonathan was struck by how sad she looked. He registered she'd greeted him in Finnish. He wished he could speak Finnish. That's why he was here, to pick her brains, to benefit from her knowledge.

He was admitted into a hall with a chequered floor – it was archetypal, somehow, this high-ceilinged space with brass hooks for coats, and Nordic touches: Marimekko fabric stretched over a frame to add splashes of careful colour. It was nice.

'Jonathan,' he said. Why not Jon? the voice said, in his head. Because I'm a grown-up, I like it, he replied.

Always this unease. Always. Had it always been there, or was he now imposing it?

How did he recall himself, before, as a child? *I lived in a tree-lined street in suburbia,* he might say – a cliché. Why was he obsessed with cliché? In his own case, it was as if he desired to airbrush his experience so it conformed to dominant patterns.

There was a cherry tree right in front of the house. In spring, pink blossom would fill the window of his parents' bedroom. *I remember gazing raptly at all that pink one day, leaning on tiptoe against the sill, which pressed hard into my chest. I was wearing dungarees with a train embroidered onto the front. My Dad said, 'Like the pink, do you?'*

I'm so self-conscious when I try to narrate. I wish I could be like him*: strong, self-assured. He doesn't seem to care what others think. Is that strength, I sometimes wonder, or is it arrogance?*

Perhaps he should remember the pink blossom more, and the shadows on the walls of his bedroom, fluttering curtains: the banal beauty of English suburban life. Barbecue smoke in summer, cars coughing painfully into life in winter. The world was clearly delineated, in that patch of London: school, doctor, dentist. Bus trips to the nearby shopping centre for shoes and clothes. Nothing to complain about.

But a stifling of a shadowy dancing presence at the edge of things, beyond the neatly ordered lawns and brick boxes with their master bedrooms and nurseries.

I tried to tell *him* about it, on the balcony of his swish, waterside flat. The conversation fell flat, though, and I wondered why I'd even tried to start it.

He just glided through life; nothing stuck to him, seemingly. It's the art of living smoothly. Somehow he's mastered it, being inured to ordinary slights and hurts.

Jonathan pictured himself, a sandy-haired boy at the seaside, whose bucket and spade were swept away by the great grey waves, crying helplessly to see them go. His father's voice stabbing at him.

His great-great-great-grandmother was Finnish, and an artist, and married to an artist. He didn't know Finnish. His parents were not artists, and he was a would-be one, a young one. And why? Why did some people want to make art, where for others nothing could be further from their thoughts? A curse, a bourgeois privilege, or both?

Anyway, she had become a talisman, this figure – taliswoman? She was on Wikipedia, in Finnish. Eino S., his great-great-great-grandfather has a much more detailed Wikipedia page, in many languages. There was a link to the museum in his house. Jonathan would love to go. He found himself looking at pictures of it, wishing someone would take him, his ex? He wished himself out of the flat he was living in above the loud Ethiopian restaurant, with the flatmates who were random, sometimes even hostile.

He had found himself assembling a sort of collage of stuff relating to Finland in the late nineteenth century. Information about Anna was scarce; he came upon a couple of short, fairly dismissive references to her in books about the Golden Age of Finnish art, but then he found another book which had reproductions of some of her works, which were held in various private collections in Finland.

He tried to learn the language, but it was too hard. Then someone told him about Emma. It frustrated him, his ignorance. Who was Anna? *I can never know. I can get an idea, maybe, especially if I carry on learning the language. I think that's what really gets to me. How much we don't know. How can we bear it? I mean, I suppose we just trick ourselves quite a lot into thinking we do know stuff. We only see colour out of a small part of our eye, and the brain colours the rest.*

And she lived on this 'leafy street in North London', with her chequered hall with its brass hooks. Jonathan, having rushed from the tube, arrived sweaty and breathless. She was a stout woman in an orange jumper. She was calm and welcoming with her Finnish salutation (but so sad). She showed Jonathan into the kitchen, which had red tiled flooring, and served him tea made of colourless, tasteless leaves in a chunky, misshapen mug. Jonathan wondered if she had made it herself, the mug. The house was high-ceilinged and spacious. The sort in which children's voices once echoed, a dog's bark, in the evenings, the tinkling of wine glasses and the bray of educated voices.

She set down some biscuits on the pitted old table and ran her chunky fingers through her hair, which stood up. She was wearing an amber necklace with her cowl-necked jumper.

He polished off the biscuit and washed it down with some of the liquid. Emma pushed the plate towards him again, and he took another oaty disc.

A clock ticked from the wall. Jonathan could see a small lawn beyond the window and a massive oak tree. They talked about Anna S., urgently at first, then they relaxed; then they moved to wine. Emma was writing a book about Anna – it was in note-form at the moment but getting there.

He felt somehow ashamed when she asked him about his project. 'Not much to tell, as yet.'

'My daughter studied art too,' she said at one point. Then her face shut down. Very suddenly. She poured more wine.

Later, she said in her accented voice, mouth by now dark red with wine, 'I will never regret having children.'

'Of course,' he said politely, swiftly, slightly shocked by the shadowy underside of this statement. (Why would you?)

'No,' she says, and her eyes stare out of her face, two great pools, brimming with feeling.

He made a non-committal face, felt himself do it. Childbearing couldn't be further from his thoughts – he thought, child; child, borne, as are we all, we shadows, we flesh.

'Life,' the woman, Emma, said. 'Life is all there is, all we are. Life. Vita.'

Then, later on: '*Ars longa, vita brevis.*'

'We are shadows,' put in Jonathan.

He noticed a biography of Virginia Woolf on the shelf.

'Did *you* know Shakespeare was a woman?' Emma said at some point.

'Er...'

'Shakes-beard,' she said, as if to clinch her argument.

He thought she was joking.

She lifted up an empty bottle of wine. '*In vino veritas*?' he queried. She gave him a sideways smile.

Emma sent Jonathan off on his way then, as if he were a boy headed for school, he thought. There were some men's coats hanging from the hooks by the door.

*

Emma's husband had gone away and left her. Left her, she cried in her head. Like a dog, she often thought, in line with Kafka, though the link wasn't quite clear in her mind. But there was something of the animal about it; she was like a large beast – say an overgrown guinea pig, parted hair in the middle of its back – left alone in its stable. He'd gone to a new stable, a tiny diddy one, very chic, a mews house, where they used to keep horses, didn't you know? Or was it birds of prey? Gone to a snickering, taloned woman called Clara or something. Who was 'actually really lovely', people said, of course they did. And she, toxic witch, or old abandoned animal – or else, why not, dignified rock, statue, posed here, unmoving, just watching, mind ticking over (if not heart – heart very quietly murmuring, still going, still alive, alive-oh).

She went often to the National Gallery, ignoring the women with their tablets, urging her to press a button on the screen – £10, £15, £20 – and instead shoving a creased note into the slot, in the huge plastic money box, occasionally, if she felt like it. 'Just popping in.' She looked at Van Gogh's grass, painted while he was in the asylum, remembered herself, lying in grass as a child, or young person, in Finland, fragrant, intricate grass; smelling, seeing, feeling it. Poor Vincent, magnificent Vincent, brave Vincent. Who was she to venture to label him? The grass, so verdant, so there. She wondered at it, again and again; how well preserved it was. In the newspaper one day, she read an article about Vincent in the asylum; they'd found the visitors' book. She could not paint, herself, but was fascinated by those who could.

'Opportunity for growth,' Emma said out loud into the ticking kitchen. A photo of her daughter stared down at her from the corkboard. Emma stared back at it for a moment, then got up and went to her study.

*

Jonathan couldn't stop thinking about his ancestral house, and he bought the books that featured it and gazed at the charming domestic scenes. He had to make his ignorant fascination part of the whole project, he realised, but how? Colouring in the world, blissfully ignorant. (Using mirrors, along with archival material?) Emma sent him a postcard from the house, where she travelled for research (she'd been before, of course, but wanted to go again): 'Greetings from X. The mosquitoes are tormenting me, but the lake is lovely and mirror-calm.'

They had lunch again; salmon and a rocket salad. And there was white wine, crisp and cold, and a basket of poppy-seeded rolls. Jonathan felt like a little boy, as he sat there waiting for Emma to bring the food over. One day, he thought, I'll have a place of my own I can invite people to, make them comfortable in.

Emma told him about the house. She'd had to put on felt slippers over her shoes, to protect the floor, she said. 'It was boiling inside,' Emma commented, lifting her glass. She patted a leaflet lying next to her plate, slid it over. 'I bought this for you. There was a little shop – or anyway, table, with postcards and Eino's books for sale.

'The family moved out of the house around 1910. After that, Eino just used it occasionally for painting and parties. He died an old man, as you'll know. By then he was living in Helsinki. I went to see the villa he lived in.'

'Really?' Jonathan asked. He felt breathless. Strangely excited.

'I've got some photos on the computer. Would you like to see?'

So he went upstairs with her, right up to the attic: a massive room filled with books and a large desk in front of a window. She switched on her computer. 'Slow,' she said, sitting down heavily on the orthopaedic chair. She gestured to a stool, on which Jonathan duly perched. She was wearing a green tunic today, and some chunky beads.

She showed him pictures of the museum and Eino's villa. Then she gestured to a pile of books she was using for research. 'Have a look at them,' she said. 'I'll get coffee.'

He leafed through the books. Eino's sugary pictures, other painters. He liked Helena W.'s bold yet nuanced work. He looked around for a moment, taking in the enviable room, and caught sight of a photo of a girl in a silver frame. It was partly covered by the curtain, so he reached out and unveiled it. It showed a healthy-looking girl, red-cheeked and smiling in her navy uniform. She looked a bit like Emma.

He was just opening a dusty pamphlet when Emma came into the room with a tray. She nodded permission or encouragement at him. The reproductions inside were in black and white – some still lifes and a landscape – delicate but strong. There was a portrait of a child.

'Her younger sister,' Emma said. 'She'd stopped painting by the time she had her own children.'

'The paintings are in private collections,' she said. 'But I saw one, in a tiny museum outside Helsinki.' She described taking the bus and then having to walk through pine trees to reach the house, at the edge of a lake. She showed Jonathan which painting she had seen, using the pamphlet.

'And what does it say about her life?' He nodded at the book, wishing once again that he could understand Finnish.

'Very little. It just says she was married to Eino and had children.'

A sleek black cat came into the room and miaowed pointedly. 'Let's go downstairs.'

In the kitchen, Jonathan watched Emma put food into the cat's bowl. 'Do you live here alone?'

'No,' she said. 'There's this one, too. Puss. Shall we have some more wine? Or do you need to get back?'

'No. I don't need to get back.'

Emma said she was thinking of going back to Finland, buying a small flat in Helsinki near the sea, where she could cycle along the shore and go regularly to sauna, and... But it none of it seemed quite convincing. 'I live here,' she declared, 'in the hotchpotch, the clutter, the ugliness, the variety of London, which grounds me. And there is my daughter, of course, though she's grown up – middle-aged now, really.'

She told him how it felt, to go back to Finland; and about gaining access to archives and private collections, the ruses she had had to use.

*

Back in Helsinki again for a funeral, Emma stepped out into the fresh spring air, pulling her jacket around her. She took a bus, for the sake of prudence, and stared out of the window at the pines and retail outlets, and a new development that was like a toy-town: all colourful houses.

She had dinner with her friend, who was sunk in grief, having lost her husband. Emma's hotel was on the sixth floor of a building, and her small, plain room led directly off the reception area. She put on the television and sipped the whisky she bought from Alko earlier. She went to sleep and dreamt she was being bound to a bunk. She was screaming, but no sound came out of her mouth. She woke up clammy and troubled.

In the morning, she breakfasted in a nearby café: Karelian pie with egg-butter on top. Two cups of strong coffee. She resisted the cinnamon buns she had always loved. Her waist was no longer extant.

The funeral was a blur. She felt battered, desolate, recalling the friend she had lost, remembering his wryness, his gentleness. The loss was hard to grasp.

The collector was a grey-haired woman, very upright and with striking blue eyes and a turquoise silk scarf knotted around her neck, and crisp navy trousers. Ecco shoes and a light, Chinese-style jacket completed the look. They drove along a track, passing letter boxes on sticks, detached wooden houses, until eventually the collector, Maria, turned into the yard of an imposing white wooden villa.

Emma followed her hostess in taking off her shoes and walking down a low-ceilinged passageway, painted a blue-grey colour. They came to a kitchen: large, bright, with a wooden table and benches, pots of herbs, a big range with crocheted pot holder dangling from hooks next to it. There were smeary children's pictures up on the cupboards; they stood out as garish amidst the muted colours of the rest of the room.

'Go through,' the collector said, nodding at a door. Emma found herself in a glassy space filled with white wicker furniture. It overlooked a long garden filled with berry bushes and fruit trees that sloped down to a lake. A boat lay upended by a small jetty that pointed out into the calm water.

Coffee and buns. Maria explained she was an artist herself, once. She had long admired the work of Helena W. and had done some research on her contemporaries, including Anna S. 'Shall we go and see?'

Again Emma followed her, this time to a large, high-ceilinged room, with formal, old-looking furniture. And on an easel was the picture she had seen previously only in reproduction, in that slim book she found in Helsinki. It was a portrait of a girl, the artist's sister. It showed promise, especially in its handling of light.

Emma ended up staying the night. Following a meal over wine, and in the flickering light of a candle, a mosquito-spiral burning nearby, they talked about female artists of the period and Emma's book.

The hospital was on an island, reachable by ferry. It was a hotel now. There was a wedding in progress. Emma caught a glimpse of the happy couple coming through an archway thronged by well-dressed well-wishers. There was an information hut in a pink wooden construction with assorted maps and leaflets, and a tiny café – just a couple of round wooden chairs and stools – and she bought a coffee, which she drank out of a paper cup with awkward handles, and a bright-pink-iced bun, sugary and reviving after last night's brandy. She read in a leaflet about the history of the hospital, which had admitted its last patients in the early 1960s. There was little information about the treatments meted out here.

But a young man, a gangly student, was giving tours of the island. She was his only customer, and she followed him round with interest. He showed her a narrow room in the hotel that had once been used for patients. She stood in the middle of it, imagining, trying to imagine Anna here. The young man knew about her, she was surprised to learn. He was a history student. He knew about the treatments, too: he mentioned baths, rest, occupation. He said he could investigate Anna S. for her. She gave him her card. She doubted he'd find anything but was gladdened by the shared interest.

Back on the mainland, in the nearest large town, she checked into a clean, quiet hotel and headed for the library to read a PhD thesis written a few years ago about the island she had just visited.

Afterwards, she lay on the bed swigging whisky recklessly from a miniature bottle she'd got on the plane. She had been feeling dizzy all day.

Her table was in the corner of the hotel restaurant, which was simply and unaffectedly decorated, with bunches of wildflowers adorning the tables, and by a window. It looked out to the sea, all glowing and blue in the evening sun that had just seen fit to break out from the grey clouds.

Emma opted for pikeperch and a carafe of white. She didn't have much of an appetite and only picked at the fish. The wine was good, and she enjoyed the soothing feeling it brought to her stomach. She was drinking more. She noted that to herself, of herself, in the third person. The view from the window really was lovely.

Her gaze roamed the walls and was brought up short by a painting of an upturned boat, by water. There was a familiarity about its technique, its sensibility. She felt like getting out her phone to take a picture of it, but she sensed she should be discreet. She also had a mind to ring someone – the collector? Jonathan?

She looked. Deep browns, blues, greens, the colours laid on slab-like, blockish, but suggesting still the play of light, the breeze. There were leaf-patterned shadows on the shore; grass; rock; then the water, blue and white, evoking the ceaseless movement of the lake, plashing at the rocks.

The oars were laid out by the boat, seeming to invite one to take them up and row off.

The distant shore was suggested by an olive-green, smudgy line, and then above that, the sky, a brilliant blue.

Outside the window, sea was lapping at the stony shore.

She finished her wine and went up to her room, which was small, like the one she had seen on the tour, but pleasant: clean, furnished in light colours. She sat on the bed, feeling breathless and restless. She knew what she would do.

In the early hours, she crept downstairs. There was no one at reception, but a doorway led from the area behind the desk to a room that was lighted. Probably someone was about. She crept into the dining room and went over to the painting. She reached up and lifted it from its hook. There was no signature and no sticker marking on the back. It would fit in her case, she judged.

So she took it up to her room and placed it on the bed. Then she set out on another exploratory journey. This took her to the kitchens and the basement. The dark, echoey spaces down there were gloomy, rather eerie. She came upon the laundry room, storage spaces, the wine cellar. No more paintings.

Only in the morning, when she woke to see the painting propped up against the wall opposite her, did it occur to her she could just have asked the manager about the painting, rather than making off with it.

She went down to breakfast, the better not to attract suspicion, meanwhile covering the painting with dry towels and putting the 'Do Not Disturb' sign on the door. Breakfast was a lavish buffet. She managed some scrambled eggs and coffee. She didn't dare look at the empty rectangular space where the painting had used to hang, at first, but when she finally did, she was surprised to see it had already been replaced. Was a search of the rooms underway? Had the police been alerted? Would she soon be escorted out of the breakfast room, 'taken for questioning'? The replacement was an insipid watercolour of a forested landscape.

Breakfast over, she was faced with the dilemma of whether or how to get the painting out of the hotel unnoticed.

She packed it in her suitcase and checked out, breathless.

'What have I done?' she asked the dealer on the phone that evening.

Maria registered that it was the woman from London, who professed to have made off with a painting. She sounded rather confused.

Maria established her whereabouts. It turned out she was nearby, in a kiosk, sheltering from the rain, she said.

Maria sighed. 'Do you have anywhere to stay?'

'No,' came the answer, timidly hopeful.

'Okay, stay there. I'll come.' Maria exited into the rain.

She pulled up at the kiosk. It was bright, and like a Hopper painting, with the single form standing in the doorway: a picture of isolation.

Emma looked sheepish and bedraggled. The women walked quickly out into the night, and Maria placed Emma's case in the boot.

At the house, they sat down in the kitchen, and Maria made tea. She fetched rum and held the bottle quizzically over the steaming cups. Emma nodded gratefully. Her face was red, and her eyes shone out, hectic and excited.

The painting leant against the wall. They both stared at it, and then Emma explained.

'You stole it,' Maria said finally.

They stared at each other, then Emma looked away.

Maria began to laugh.

After a while, she poured out more tea and rum. A candle flickered on the table.

Maria made up a bed for Emma in the same room where she stayed last time, while Emma hovered in the doorway, expressing thanks.

Maria said good night and went down to the kitchen, where she sat staring at the canvas.

*

Jonathan was now fascinated by spaces, he had decided. It was living in that flat; it had given him a heightened awareness of how the body extended into space, or remained confined. How we use objects to orient ourselves. He was so cramped, so stifled by the sounds others made. Then there was social or public space; the way some actions were allowed to take place, and others were hidden away. And the way that was enforced: not always explicitly. And he liked the shadows and the margins.

Emma wanted to meet up. At first, he didn't feel like it, having moved on from his project about Anna S., well, abandoned it, really. But he remembered sitting in her study, and the photo of her daughter, for some reason, and then the whole project, and he agreed, suggesting a café.

She told him about the painting; it was with a collector now.

'So what?' he said. 'You stole it?'

'Well, retrieved,' she said. She shifted. 'Anyway, it will all get sorted. I'll clear it with them.'

'Okay,' he said, with a little laugh.

His phone buzzed; it was his mother, and he felt himself involuntarily grimace.

'Everything all right?' asked Emma.

'Oh, my flat,' he said. 'I'm having some issues.' He tried to sound casual. 'So I rang my mother.' He was behind with his rent. He realised how absolutely humiliating it was to be him, at the moment, how thrown upon circumstance. No money, no boyfriend, and his parents not exactly wealthy, and not willing to 'fund his lifestyle'. His mind whirred with impossible options, as it had been doing for nights now.

'You could stay at mine, if you like,' she said.

He stared at her and nearly laughed again. 'Really?'

'Yes,' she replied firmly. 'Just while you look for somewhere else.'

'Okay,' he said. 'Thank you.'

So then he was there, in a small room up in the eaves, across from the study where he had sat that time. It was not quite what he had planned for his life, but it was quiet. Blissfully so. He listened to himself breathe; it was luxurious. There was a small bathroom on his floor – just a toilet and sink. He felt like he was in a boarding house early in the last century. There were rules. No visitors allowed, no being noisy, no coming in late, no smoking etc. Emma had delivered all these with a worried air. He wondered if she was regretting the invitation. But anyway, he was here, for a time, and he could smell food. He realised he should go and buy something to eat. He had seen a shop on the corner.

There was a knock at the door. 'Come in,' he replied unnaturally.

Emma, looking flushed and wearing a stained blue-and-white-striped apron, asked him, 'Would you like to join me for food?'

She asked this formally, not looking at him directly, and he noticed her Finnish accent particularly this time.

'Nice to cook for someone,' she said downstairs. 'Occasionally,' she added, unscrewing a bottle of red wine and pouring some into both their glasses without asking.

Jonathan felt awkward with gratitude and over-praised everything: the wine, the meaty lasagne, the flowers on the side.

'My daughter brought them round,' Emma said.

'Oh, nice.' He waited.

Emma's lips were stained with purple. She must have had some wine while cooking. 'She was in a cult,' she said. She shrugged, and her eyes look suddenly wet and pouchy.

'I'm sorry,' Jonathan said.

She shrugged again. 'You can't control people. You can't even really know them.' She said with force. 'Anyway, at least she came today.'

'True,' he said, hearing his high, reedy voice and wincing.

'They've decided not to press charges, the hotel. But they have taken their painting back.'

'Fair enough,' he observed. He began to relax, then, what with the food and wine, and the promise of somewhere quiet to sleep. It was a temporary solution, but there were only ever temporary solutions, weren't there?

Later, Emma went and got a tart, pear, from the large, retro-style fridge.

'Not home-made,' she commented.

'Shall I cook tomorrow?' he asked.

'Can you?' She narrowed her eyes.

He nodded.

'So the painting's back in the hotel,' he prompted a little later. They were in the sitting room now, at the front of the house. It had an unused feel and smelt of leather and dust.

Emma held up her glass of brandy to the light, admiring it. She nodded. 'By the way, do you need to ring your parents, let them know where you are?'

'I'll do it tomorrow. My number hasn't changed...'

'Yes, I suppose we're all mobile today. But anyway, yes, the painting's back where it was. The owner says it's alarmed now so no one can just walk off with it.' She broke off and made a funny face, stretching her mouth downwards as far as it could go and rolling her eyes. Rueful.

'I still wonder if there's any other work, but probably not. The whole place was evacuated when the Russians came to the area in 1939. I suppose a lot of stuff just got lost or destroyed at that point. Assuming they'd been kept that long.

And there's no record of her painting after she left. But you never know.'

Jonathan glanced at the clock, suddenly feeling a little oppressed by all this, he didn't know, history? Connectivity? Anyway, he needed to get up for work.

He told her about the job in the bookshop. It had given him enough money for rent, but he'd had to let the studio go. He had a storage container with all his stuff in it, but he couldn't work there. Emma looked concerned. 'Will you be able to work here? While you're staying, I mean?'

He was touched. He patted her shoulder as he passed her to go upstairs.

Jonathan had been asked to join a project on 'family lines' at a former garage in Kings Cross. It was a whitewashed space, right by a railway line; trains sent shudders through the whole place at regular intervals. He was glad to be asked; it meant somebody had noticed his work, actually registered its themes. There were about ten of them, different ages and backgrounds.

He told Emma about it over breakfast. He never used to eat breakfast, but he did now, at Emma's. He shouldn't get too comfortable here.

You just have to sort of carry on, don't you? That's what he thought, trudging along Emma's street to the tube station in the drizzle, on the way to work. Every day try to do something useful, something that brings you further towards the self you'd like to be. Is this the wisdom of age? he wondered. He still knew bugger all, but maybe he now knew something: you just carried on. Much of life was just that, tiny incremental developments, if any: not spectacular happenings.

When he got back from the shop, tired, Emma seemed to be thinking similar things. She sighed as she set down her mug of herbal tea and said, 'Well, tomorrow I'm back to work. On the book,' she added. 'About your great-great-great-grandmother.'

'Well that's good, isn't it?' he sat down on the bench and drank his own tea.

'Yes,' she said, joining him at the table. 'It is. It's a great privilege.'

Jonathan thought about his parents, who seemed to value nothing more than routine. He realised, though, that he probably had an ageist view of older people as fixed and settled. Emma was looking at him, smiling. He flushed and changed the subject but was interrupted by a knock at the door. Emma got up and went to the door, from where murmuring noises reached him.

A moment later, Emma came in, followed by a younger woman, who he guessed, from her resemblance to the photo in the study, was Laura, her daughter.

'Laura, this is Jonathan. Jonathan, Laura.' Emma seemed quite calm, but her eyes had widened oddly.

He stood clumsily, managing to bang his shin on a table leg. He shook the hand of the woman, who looked at him quite blankly. She was wearing plain, dark clothes and no make-up. Her round face was severe-looking, serious, and her hair was chin-length. She didn't look outlandish or mad, as he supposed he might have expected.

He made his excuses and went up to his room, where he made some notes for the Family Lines project. He started drifting off, thinking of one of the participants, Georg.

*

Emma looked at the young woman in her kitchen. Her hair was tangled, and she itched to sit her down and take a comb to it.

She remembered the smell of the lotion they bought for nits. Laura had been a calm, stoical child; at least that's how she seemed. Emma was too ready to accept this version of the girl that she presented to her. She could reproach herself endlessly. She should... what? Not have worked? Hovered over her, waiting to probe and pry? She really didn't think that would have helped. But perhaps one always finds ways of excusing oneself.

It was so hard, looking back, to pull out the relevant points, the noteworthy details. The past was a blur. And of course life itself, experience, was a headlong rush through and into the unknown. Sometimes it seemed we glimpsed some fundamental truth, but that, too, could slip through one's hands.

Emma had thought the fundamental truth was that Laura was her daughter, and they would always be bound by that blood-tie, whatever differences there may be between them. But when she dropped out of university and took up with that cult, Emma faltered in this belief. Laura became distant, rarely phoning. When she did consent for Emma to visit her, it was in cafés near the place she was living, and she was shifty and evasive. Emma remembered the Formica tables and posters of sausages skewered by forks, the builders and cabbies devouring bacon and eggs, the misted-up windows. Herself, hapless and hopeless, a supplicant for her daughter's attention.

Laura grew thinner and paler and more guarded. Emma read up on cults, of course she did. Laura's was presided over by some guru. 'Guru!' Emma said once; it burst out of her against her will. She knew it would antagonise Laura, and it did; she got up and left minutes later.

More than anything, Emma was and remained frightened by how manipulable we are. Anyone can just come along and wash our brains, remove our will. It happened all the time, in innumerable variants. Many marriages are forms of cults, including her own. Theirs was founded on the cult of culturedness. They were a cultured couple, concealing their own banality – in particular his masculine self-importance, her feminine masochism – by an emphasis on their educatedness. They were opera-lovers (he was, Emma never liked it), museum-visitors. Her Finnishness added a touch of exoticism, but not too much, for she was an anglicised Anglophile, respectable. A settled alien.

The marriage foundered in the years after Laura joined the cult. She left it eventually – Emma gathered the whole thing dissolved – but still never 'came back' to them, if she was ever with them truly. That girl whose hair she combed – did she ever know what was going on in her head?

Laura stood there now in the kitchen and glanced at her. Emma wondered if she saw now that she was old. Just an old woman living on her own with an art student for a lodger.

Her book was nearly finished. There'd be no fanfare, of course, when it came out; it was an obscure academic book about an obscure female artist whose output was very small. There might be some interest in Finland; a friend from school had invited her to give a talk at the library in which she worked. But not much fuss around here. Still, she was pleased, even if it was only lodged for posterity in the British Library.

It was to be called: *Painting Silence: The Life and Work of Anna S.* She would send a copy to Jonathan, of course, once it was out. He was in Berlin, at the moment, living with a man called Georg. He sent her the odd email. Kind of him. Strange to think he actually lived there for six months.

She was thinking of selling up, going to Finland. She'd buy that flat near the sea, after all, and a bike, and take those walks in the bracing air, and through the snow. She loved London, but the house was too big, and somehow she felt she'd had her time there. Her marriage was well and truly in the past, she had no job to tie her there, and her daughter remained remote, however close or far they were geographically from each other. It would always be so, she just knew it.

Working on Anna had made her miss Finland. Though hers wasn't a happy story, Emma believed from the material she'd been able to access that Anna's final years were serene. She was happy in the asylum outside Helsinki, enjoying the surroundings and walks in the grounds. She was 'calm and stable', the notes said, and Emma decided to believe them. Her other life fell away: her connections, her relationships. Helena was in London with Margaret, the Englishwoman she lived with until her death, Eino ceased his visits entirely, the children grew and established their own lives.

Her book didn't go into great detail about the children; they were of course mentioned in books about their father, to which Emma referred. A biography of the children would be a good idea – but for someone else to undertake.

But back to the indexing: never her favourite feature of academic endeavour.

*

The Family Lines project was officially over, but he found himself wondering about it still, about his own family. Emma sent him her book, which he had been reading.

He laid down the volume and went round the corner to the supermarket to buy coffee – they'd run out. The street was teeming. He bought coffee and popped into the Turkish bakery next door for a feta-cheese pastry and a pizza to heat up later and eat with salad.

He checked the letterbox on the way back in: nothing. The hallway was graffitied; he liked it. He liked the high-ceilinged stairway, the spacious flat. Georg was out today, for work. He was a web designer, as well as an artist. Jonathan sat down on the couch with his coffee and took in the large main room: bare floorboards, shelving made of planks and bricks, books of photography and art. He loved it. He couldn't believe he was there sometimes. And when they were out at nights, at long trestle tables with beer, under swaying lightbulbs – on a boat or at the edge of the river or in a vast building with chandeliers and gilt-edged mirrors – and music you drowned in, and beautiful people, he felt it wasn't real, this life. How could it last? Because life was about mortgage payments, wasn't it? Eating enough veg, taking the car in for its service, dental appointments and worrying about the future.

Georg couldn't understand why he worried all the time – like now, he was worried about not being worried. It was his nature, he told Georg. He was neurotic. But he argued it made him enjoy things all the more, the fleeting pleasures.

He sipped the strong black coffee and returned to the book. He found himself wondering more and more about the children, the grandchildren. The other great-great-great-grandchildren of Anna. It was amazing how many people bred. But then of course it wasn't, because how would we all be here otherwise...? God, sometimes he sounded simple. It was just a different point of view though, wasn't it? A sort of wonder. He supposed if he were a woman, he'd at least be more aware of birth and mothering, the possibility of them, anyway. Perhaps.

So he started looking them up, his relatives. Anna's descendants. Olavi, the banker son who set up a foundation, had two sons, and one of them had four daughters, while the other had a son.

He heard the door open and felt a familiar gladdening. Georg.

'Hiii,' he called.

'Hi.' Jonathan leapt up, ready to tell him about his discovery: one of the people he was related to lived there in Berlin.

But Georg had brought someone with him, a guy they sometimes saw out at clubs. Simon, his name was. He was dark-skinned, tall, with long lashes. Jonathan didn't know where he was from, not Germany. He knew Georg liked him. His heart sank. So much for the gladdening. 'Simon's come round for drinks,' Georg said. Jonathan greeted him unenthusiastically and followed Georg into the kitchen, where he was getting out the gin and tonic. He suddenly remembered Billy.

'I thought we were staying in tonight,' he said. 'Drinks' always led to clubbing, and more. He heard himself: whining and petty.

Georg looked at him and took hold of his arms. 'I met him on the way here.'

'And he had nothing else to do?'

Georg frowned. He didn't seem to understand what Jonathan meant. He didn't know himself. He should be doing something else? Working? Being with his 'family'? Was that his suburban legacy: my fussy bourgeois proprietorial hangover? Why couldn't he just be gloriously, radically queer?

Still he couldn't pretend any more. 'I don't like this. I'm going out.'

He felt like crying as he walked through the main room and muttered something at their guest and got out of the flat.

He went to the cinema; it didn't even matter what he saw. He would just wait for them to go out and then creep back to the flat. Then what? Pack his things? Go back to England? Get a mortgage and 'start a family'?

He didn't think so. He got absorbed in the film and drank the beer he'd bought. He was feeling fine. He didn't need Georg. He didn't need anyone.

He got back to the flat. He saw the lights were on when he opened the door and listened out to see if they were still around. It was gone eleven. He'd have thought they'd have left by now.

Georg appeared.

'Where is he?' Jonathan asked, looking over his shoulder.

'I sent him off,' Georg said.

Jonathan felt like crying again – this time out of gratitude, and love.

So one of Olavi's great-great-great-granddaughters lived there, in Berlin. Looked like she was some kind of designer. He managed to find her email address, and they arranged to meet. He chose a place on Oranienburgerstrasse, where you sit on swaying, cushioned bamboo chairs.

Pia, her name was. She sat down and ordered a lime and soda, and she asked him about his life, what he was doing in Berlin. He told her a little. He said he had a flatmate.

'I was interested in my great-great-great-grandmother. Ours. Do you know anything about her?'

Pia shrugged. She was wearing a worn sweatshirt with a faded logo, tight trousers. She was studiedly casual. She had blonde hair and a Finnish nose: snub. She was tanned. They didn't look at all alike, he concluded.

'She was in a loony bin, wasn't she? Spent most of her life there.'

He frowned and took out Emma's book. 'You've seen this?'

'I heard about it,' she conceded. She took out a packet of cigarettes. 'Do you mind?'

He shook his head and took a sip of beer. A knot of tourists passed, maps in hand. 'Did you know anything about your great-great-grandfather?' he asked. 'Olavi.'

'Not really. But he was quite well known in Finland. Because of the foundation he set up, for women artists. His grandson leads it now, my— *our* grandfather – though he's getting quite old now.'

'Where does he live?'

'Near Helsinki.'

Pia finished her drink. 'Well, it's been nice meeting you.' She got up. 'I've got somewhere I need to be.'

'Oh, no problem.' He stood up and found himself offering his hand. Then she went off down Oranienburgerstrasse. That was that. He sat in the darkening evening, as people passed by, shouting, laughing, ready for the night ahead. He stared over at Tacheles, the deliberate bohemianism of its peeling, shabby facade. He was thinking about his great-great-grandfather and his foundation. Eventually he got up and walked home, past the sex workers and nightclubbers and tourists.

When he got in, he sat in the glow of the laptop. Georg was out with some people from work. He enjoyed the stillness of the flat, just the rumble of traffic and the noises of the night coming from outside. Dull booming sounds, occasional shouts and laughs. He composed an email message to Emma, telling her about his meeting with Pia.

He received an email back almost immediately. Emma must be at her desk. She gave her phone number, asked if he could call her.

Just then the door opened, and Georg called out, 'Hi'. Jonathan could tell immediately he'd had a bit to drink. He came in with a sloppy smile on his face, swaying slightly. 'Whatcha doing in the dark?' he slurred indignantly.

He leant over and switched on the nearby lamp and went over and hugged him. He was full of gossip about the evening, but Jonathan made him sit down while he put some coffee on and brought him a pint-glass of water. He forgot about Emma as they sat entangled and he told him about his evening and grew sentimental.

He found an email from Emma in his inbox the next day: 'I suppose you didn't get my message. Ring me when you get the chance!'

He rang. There'd been a discovery.

*

Emma received an email from the young man who had given her the guided tour of the island. He said he had found something, and could he speak to her? He was very mysterious about it, very hush-hush. He said he was in London. She was a bit suspicious but agreed to meet him in the British Museum. They sat under the bright dome in the dazzling space, on uncomfortable benches. Emma bought them coffee.

'I've been thinking of moving to Finland,' she said. 'So you're lucky to have caught me here. What are you doing here?' In fact, she'd been dithering over her move so much that really and truly – she knew it then – it wasn't going to happen. Fine.

'I'm on a visit,' he explained. 'I saved up, from my holiday job. I love the museums.' He looked up and around and smiled, with wonder. He listed the museums he'd visited. She watched him, touched.

Then he stopped and fixed on her. 'Before I left, though, I searched the hotel. I had a feeling there'd be something else. I read your book, and...'

'And?'

The boy had gone red. He fidgeted with his wooden coffee stirrer, setting it down finally next to the torn-open sugar sachets on the tray. 'I'm going to write about Anna for my thesis. I read your book.'

'Well,' she said, 'I'm flattered.'

'It's because of the hotel, the connection...' He frowned and looked to the side. He really was very shy. She patted his hand. 'Yes,' she said. 'I can see how that would be.'

'Anyway,' he said, as if he hadn't heard her. 'I found something.'

'Yes?' she asked, encouragingly. 'Where?'

He told her he went to the second asylum, where Anna lived until her death. He looked at the records, as had Emma, found nothing much of interest, just bland, factual notes on Anna's behaviour, which had been consistently 'good': calm and docile. She had appeared to enjoy walks in the grounds and occasionally handicrafts.

'I gained permission to visit the place. It's a school now, for disabled children. Nice,' he added.

She nodded. She had seen the school's website: bright, attractive rooms, spacious grounds, kind-looking staff, and children engaged in a wide range of activities.

'Anyway, I sort of asked them to let me look in the attic space. They have a huge storage area up there.'

'Uh-huh.' She took a sip of coffee, deliberately calm. She didn't question his methods, her own having been somewhat unorthodox. 'And?' she had to prompt. He was being deliberately slow with his revelation, whatever it was.

He leant forward and whispered. 'Paintings!'

She stared at him. To his credit, he didn't keep her dangling much longer. He whipped out his mobile phone, which had a large screen. Perhaps it wasn't a phone at all. Anyway, whatever it was, it flashed up images, one after the other, which she drank in. The surroundings receded, the school party at the next table, the mothers and their toddlers, the tourists, and she saw only the images, a dozen of them at least: landscapes, mainly, lovely. Water framed by red berries, a black bird seen from the side. A rowing boat, but this one in the water, seen as if from the rower's viewpoint, just the tip, and the water, rippling, and the dark forest edging the shore. Then a snowy scene: branches dripping with white, a dark and brooding sky...

'Amazing,' she whispered. She looked at the young man. 'This... is... amazing!'

He had gone red again, right to the tips of his ears, and his eyes gleamed. He looked almost handsome, in this state of pleasure and suppressed excitement. 'I knew you'd be pleased,' he said.

'Pleased!' she cried out. 'I'm...' But she couldn't think of the word. She got up, for some reason. 'This calls for a celebration!' Then questions occurred to her, and she sat back down again.

'Where are the paintings now? Who knows about them? We have to handle things carefully, make sure they're looked after...'

'I spoke to the director of the school about them. She said she'd been meaning to get someone to look at them at some point. I said I thought they might be significant, and I have contacts, and she agreed to keep them in there while I sorted it out. I thought I'd tell you first, as I was coming to London anyway.'

'Well I'm very glad you did.' Her thoughts were racing. She had wild visions of nocturnal break-ins, ladders made of tied-up sheets, moonlit drives, squealing breaks, policemen's voices issuing commands.

The boy was looking at her. She wondered what he had been envisaging.

'I think we should go via a more official route than I did last time. Don't you?'

The boy's shoulders slumped a little, with disappointment or relief, she couldn't tell. She started thinking aloud – they should contact Maria, the collector, of course, who would know the best way of storing the paintings and valuing them. And then she supposed she should contact the family. Maybe the foundation could put on an exhibition. She started to grow excited. 'Yes. An exhibition, and a related programme of events. Lectures, talks... And I'll have to revise my book,' she said, smiling. 'I just hope I live long enough!' she added jocularly, looking again at the images on the phone-thing.

The boy stiffened, silent. He made a concerned face.

'Oh, don't worry,' she said. 'Nothing serious.'

Just a few funny things she didn't want to dwell on. Anyway, there was too much to do now.

'We have to get going, anyway!' she said. The boy nodded, apparently in agreement with her plan of action.

'Tell you what, your thesis will be hard to beat, with this inside story... Amazing,' she said again. 'Amazing that she produced this, in those last years... I wonder how it came about... Shall we go to a pub? Then we make a list of things to do.'

The boy agreed, and she bought herself a gin and tonic, and him a beer, which he sipped gingerly. She wondered how old he was, suddenly worried. But no, he was at university, so of course this was fine. She wasn't corrupting innocents.

They drew up their list, she scrawling on the back of an envelope, he dutifully typing it into his device.

We are all shadows, but traces will remain – echoes, shadows, reverberations.

The paintings have been hung perfectly. That's what they all agree: Emma and Maria, Jonathan and Georg. They are beautifully lit in a white-painted room with high windows that reveal birch-branches and summer sky. The space is thronged by visitors holding glasses and talking, and pointing, and glancing at the information sheets, and filled with their hubbub.

Emma walks slowly, occasionally pausing to catch her breath. Jonathan is concerned, but she doesn't meet his eye. Occasionally she leans into Maria, for support.

Jonathan looks over at Georg, who in turn is looking up at a painting of bright red berries: crimson spheres contrasting with the white snow coating the branches of the bush. He feels like crying and at the same time he's struck by how remarkable this whole event is; this discovery of his great-great-great-grandmother's paintings and now this event. And journalists taking photos and notes. The exhibition has already featured in magazines and on the radio. And it's thanks to Emma, and her investigations, and her book. He looks at her again and smiles. She smiles back, the pain seeming to lift from her face momentarily.

Emma feels giddy. The paintings seem to suck her in, knock her off her feet. They are so vivid. She feels, looking at the prow of the boat and the water, that she is there, lying in the vessel, feeling spray on her face. But then there is the reassuring strength of Maria's arm. And then there is the nagging pain that lifts only for moments at a time. She can see that Jonathan has registered it, but no matter.

There's that young lad, the student. She lifts her arm, and he comes over, grinning. 'How is your thesis coming along?'

'I've finished it. And I've got a job.'

'Oh?'

'In an archive, just temporary.' He starts telling her about it, and she feels herself smiling and smiling but at the same time receding, and still dimly but gladly aware of Maria's arm. Now Maria and the boy are talking, and Maria is saying all the right things. And Emma feels a wave of sentimental joy: that young men become archivists, that all this – she looks around vaguely – all this – art, culture, enterprise – will carry on.

She finds herself face to face with an old man in his wheelchair. His eyes look damp, and he reaches out his gnarled hand. 'My grandfather would like to thank you,' says a young woman who introduces herself as Pia.

'Oh really,' Emma says. 'It was nothing. I'm only too glad...' She falters, and she feels the pain rise within her. Maria leads her away, leaving the young archivist to talk to the old man. She's sitting on a chair now, in the corner, and Maria is bringing her a glass of water.

The old man dabs at his eyes with a handkerchief. Everything seems like a dream: this bright room, all these people, and the paintings, the paintings. They are so beautiful. She must have known that. She must have been happy to have seen them emerge, and known they were lovely.

'She was mad,' Jonathan hears someone say, a woman in a light cream suit. 'But she could paint.' Her companion laughs.

Jonathan thinks about his own exhibition, coming up in Tacheles in the autumn, but his thoughts are interrupted by the sound of someone tapping on glass. Then a woman begins talking. Jonathan picks out the word 'welcome' and gathers she is the director of the institute that now houses the exhibition, the home for disabled children. She speaks only briefly and is replaced by someone else, the curator of this exhibition, which will soon move to Helsinki. Georg has come over and put his hand on his shoulder.

*

Emma's house in London seems unreal. London itself seems like a dream, one she dreamt for years. Now she is sitting on a white wicker chair looking at an upturned boat and still, mirror-calm water, and this seems like all the reality she needs or can bear. Maria is bringing her some tea. Maria has said she can stay as long as she wants or needs. Wants or needs, it echoed in Emma's head. She worries occasionally about the house in London – what if something happens? What if Laura rings? But then she thinks that the house is surely just standing there squarely, the bills are all paid via direct debit, Laura hardly ever rings and would not worry if no one answered.

The water is sparkling. Through the lattice of her lashes, she sees its dazzle. The scent from the pine trees wafts towards her. This is life, she feels.

There is a figure at the water's edge. At the rim of the lake is someone. There is that story from the *Kalevala*, of Aino who fled her fate – wedding an aged man – to come upon the maidens on the rock, to whom she swam. And the rock sank down and she with it, and there she lived, forever, submerged in the waves, one of the watery maidens who flitted and danced and sang. And when Väinämöinen, to whom she had been betrothed, tried to hook her up, she transformed into a quick, silver fish and spoke to him mockingly and darted off into the element that was now her home.

Is the figure there Aino? Is she wondering whether to enter the lake? Silently, Emma urges her on. She squints into the glitter. She tries to raise her hand and call out, but she's weak, so weak.

Is it Aino? Or is it the woman in whose garden she was sitting? The glare is broken up by a dark shape coming towards her. It is the woman, what is her name? How funny, not to know the name of this kind, new friend. Emma feels herself smile. So Aino didn't go into the water, then? Or *she* did, but this woman chose not to. It is confusing, and she shuts her eyes. It is best to be in the dark while she tries to think this out.

She feels a touch on her hand. She remembers her mother, lying dying, and how even when she was insensible to all else, her fingers would curl round Emma's own like a baby's. And hearing. Hearing is the last sense to go, one of the doctors said.

Touch, breath. How glad she is to be here. How utterly happy. There is a voice in her consciousness.

Aino now merges with Anna. Both go into the water, and now she too will go into the water, and they'll be there together, the maidens, the ones who got out from the cells, the cloistered rooms, the mortgaged houses.

Yes, that was right. Emma gets up, nearly falls, then feels a steady hand underneath her arm. She must have got up from her chair and walked towards the water, and then she must have looked down. She must have looked down into the water.

Glare and glitter, and a hand underneath her. She can still see, but it's dim. She can feel, though. She can feel, and she can hear.

Was it the paintings that mattered? Yes, of course. Of course people – women – must see and they must share what they see...

Review of *Painting Silence*

This study by Emma K. traces the life of the hitherto largely unknown painter Anna S. As the author points out, S. has been almost exclusively discussed in relation to her famous husband Eino S., often dubbed 'Finland's Carl Larsson'. *Painting Silence* sets out to correct this bias, offering a biography of the lesser-known female artist, who led a troubled life, and analysing her connections with other artists of the period, especially Helena W.

The key fact of Anna S.'s life was her confinement to a psychiatric institution in her early thirties. K. describes the sectioning of S. as the result of 'patriarchal' power relations and of a culture that 'systematically thwarted female creativity'. She cites evidence from letters to argue that the crisis in Anna's mental health was prompted by a visit made by her friend Helena W., the successful artist, which brought to the fore various unresolved tensions in Anna's own mind, especially the denial of her creativity in favour of the drudgery and self-sacrifice bound up with marriage and motherhood. K. brings in numerous works of theory and criticism on the 'binary opposition between motherhood and creativity in Western culture', persuasively setting Anna's story in context.

Indeed, this is in general a convincing, well-written book. Nevertheless, the artistic output of its subject is small, though promising, and one wonders if this level of attention is justifiable. However, overall, this is an admirable contribution to debates concerning Nordic women artists.

There is this voice inside your head.

ALSO FROM REFLEX PRESS

Straw Gods

Tom O'Brien

Ten years after the death of her husband, Rosa struggles to move on and takes solace in rituals and superstition. Sol, a young fisherman, braves the sea to prove himself to an absent father. As a storm rips through the small community, disaster lays bare old secrets. Rosa and Sol's lives tangle in tragic circumstances, forcing them to face the truth about themselves and the ones they loved.

Straw Gods is the debut novella-in-flash from Tom O'Brien, a heart-wrenching drama both moving and exhilarating, perceptively exploring the effects of grief and the lasting bonds of family and friendship.

Straw Gods is a lyrical, fierce exploration of the dance of grief. O'Brien brings psychological depth to the characters with his understanding of the tricks of heart and minds that carry those who suffer. Unmissable.

—Stephanie Carty, *Three Sisters of Stone*

Tom O'Brien's intensely told novella examines the insularity and isolation of grief. O'Brien excels at crafting sentences that offer comfort with unembellished honesty.

—Judy Darley, *Sky, Light, Rain*

Love Stories for Hectic People

Catherine McNamara

The thirty-three flash fictions of *Love Stories for Hectic People* explore the alignment of beings that is love. There is love that is vulgar, love that knows no reason; there is love that cradles the act of living, love that springs through the cracks; love that is slaughtered. These tales take place from Italy to Ghana to Greece and London and Tokyo, in grainy cities and muted hotel rooms; there is a Mafia murder, an ambulance rescue worker and a woman whose husband falls off a mountain. There is unchaste attraction and slippery, nuanced love; police violence and porn, and fishing too.

'Catherine McNamara is one of the best writers I've read in all the time I've been in publishing.'

—Christopher James, *Jellyfish Review*

'Sharp, witty and deeply real, these small stories reveal moments of connections, and sometimes dissolution. One can't help but be captivated by these many and varied truths.'

—Michelle Elvy, *the everrumble*

Families and Other Natural Disasters

Anita Goveas

Families and Other Natural Disasters is a collection of flash fiction about families, born into, created or found, how they support us or repress us, and the ways they can change us and shape us.

These stories are set in the UK and India, in aquariums, ballrooms and outer space. They follow women into volcanoes and out to sea. The characters search for lost brothers and lost selves and find prairie dogs and sea serpents.

In a debut collection rich in cultural detail, Anita Goveas beautifully explores the theme of family as one of the essential elements that hold the universe together.

'Narratives that intersect continents, myths and folklore – a magical exploration of love, belief and the complications in relationships, with others and with oneself. Left me breathless and craving for more.'

—Susmita Bhattacharya,
The Normal State of Mind and *Table Manners*

'This gorgeous collection brims with energy and sensuality. Richly observed stories to catch the heart and quicken the pulse.'

—Sharon Telfer,
two-time winner of the Bath Flash Fiction Award

Witches Sail in Eggshells

Chloe Turner

'Witches sail in eggshells,' I heard Meg say from behind me, and I looked back. She was pounding the shells, hard, with the palm of her hand on the flat of a knife.

Perceptive, intriguing, and beautifully told, Chloe Turner's debut collection explores the themes of love, loss, the little ways we let each other down, and how we can find each other again.

'I adored this collection and know that it will take pride of place on my bookshelf. I am extremely excited to read more of Chloe Turner's work.'

—Bookish Chat

'It's been a while since I've read short stories which affected me so much. Never have I laughed, shivered and gawped so much. With Witches Sail in Eggshells Chloe Turner has made me look at short stories in a different way.'

—The Bobsphere

Some Days Are Better Than Ours

Barbara Byar

Some Days Are Better Than Ours is a startling collection that explores human life in all its forms. These stories will make you draw breath as you race through compelling accounts of the dark places people escape to and from.

Through her masterful use of language, Barbara Byar skilfully invites the reader into imagined futures and regretful pasts – from war to childhood to road trips to relationships. Her pieces are visceral, sometimes brutal but sliced through with hope. These stories, and the characters in them, strike straight at the realist heart of the human experience and will linger long after reading.

'These are searingly truthful fictions. Pitched at the border of poetry and prose, they catalogue lives lived at the edge, survivors facing the beauty and cruelty of the world. These fictions will take your breath away.'

—William Wall, *Suzy Suzy* and *Grace's Day*

'Barbara Byar writes flash like no one else; in each of these lucid and furious twenty-nine stories – some no longer than a single page – are wholly unforgettable glimpses into the lives of her individual characters.'

—Peter Jordan, *Calls to Distant Places*

REFLEX PRESS

Reflex Press is an independent publisher based in Abingdon, Oxfordshire, committed to publishing bold and innovative books by emerging authors from across the UK and beyond.

Since our inception in 2018, we have published award-winning short story collections, flash fiction anthologies, and novella-length fiction.

www.reflex.press
@reflexfiction